A SPARK IN THE DARK

PAM FONG

Greenwillow Books
An Imprint of HarperCollins*Publishers*

There is light,

and there is dark.

The light is warm and welcoming.

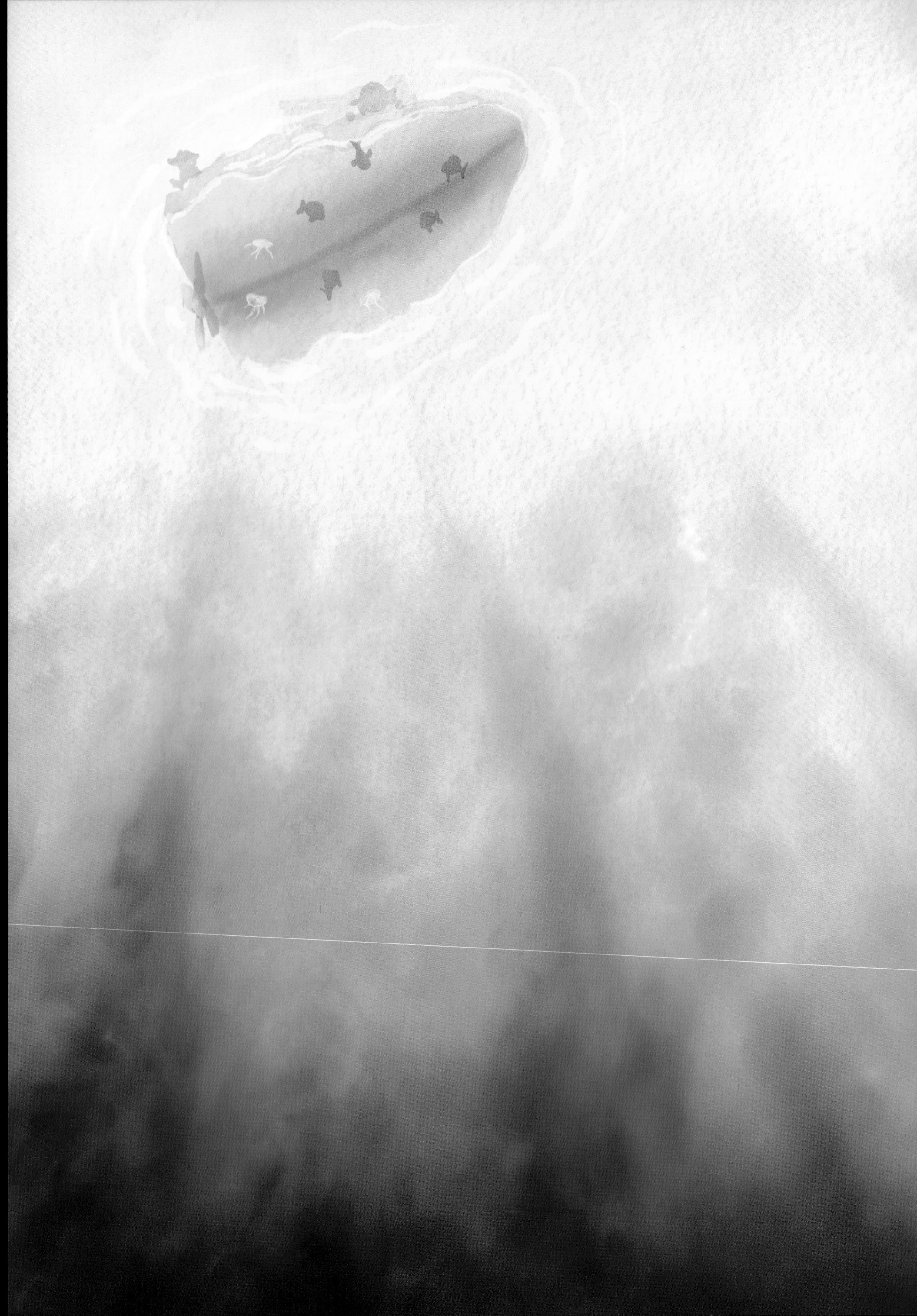

In the light, it is easy to see what's ahead.

But sometimes the dark creeps up

and surrounds you.

And before you know it . . .

there is only dark.

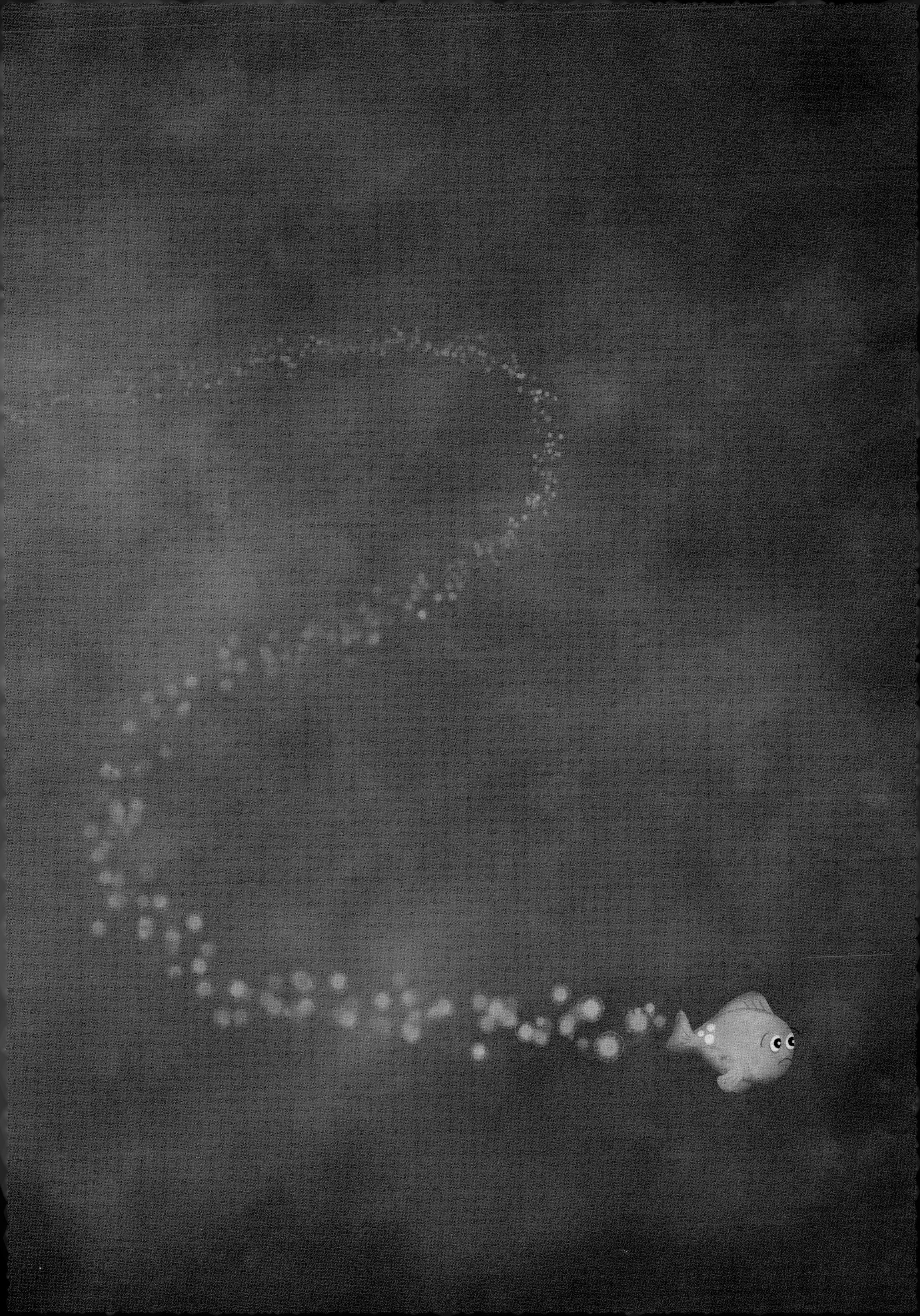

The dark can be cold, lonely, and scary.

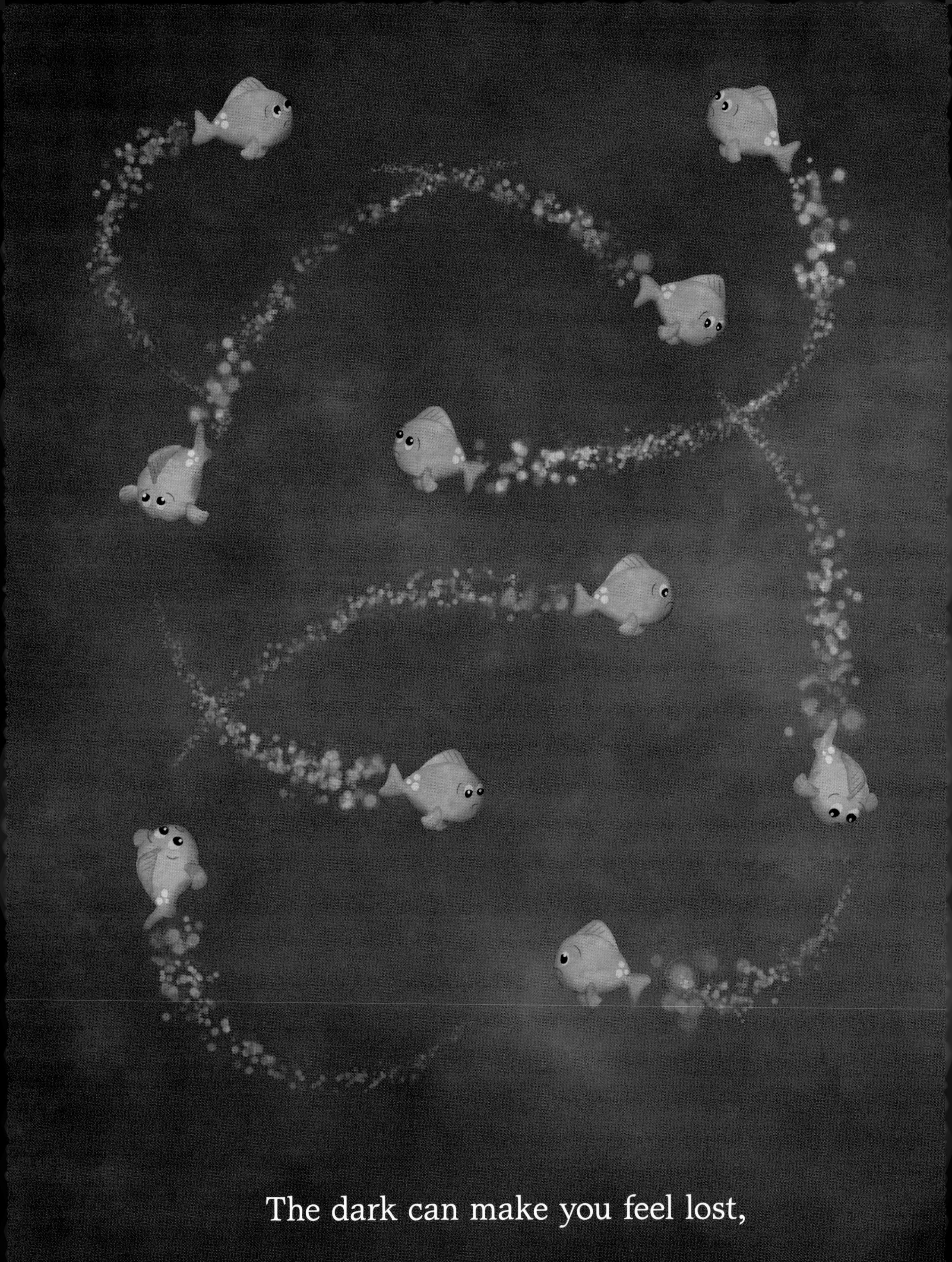

The dark can make you feel lost,

angry,

or sad.

But even in the

dark

dark

dark

light can bloom.

Then just as quickly fade away.

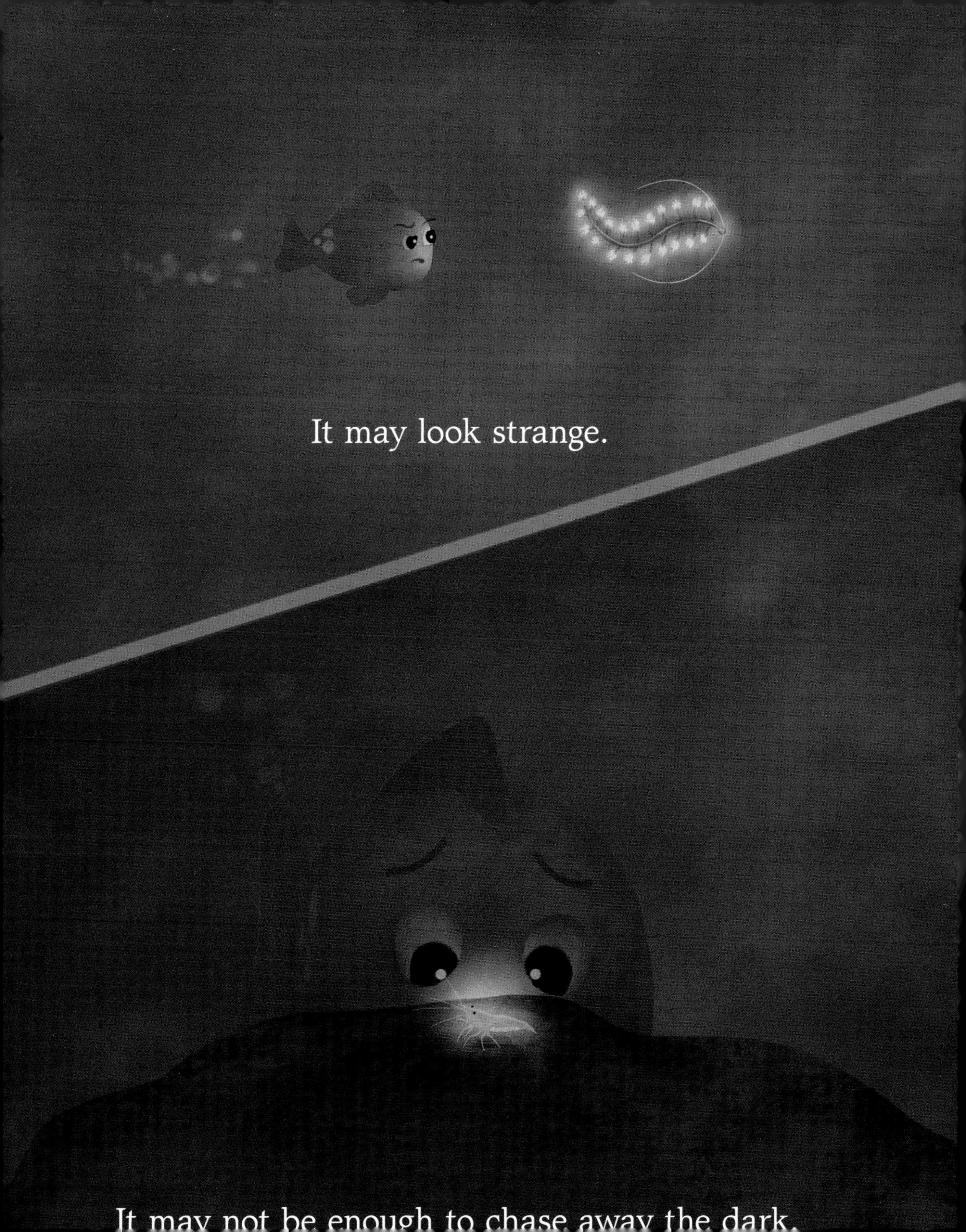
It may look strange.
It may not be enough to chase away the dark.

Sometimes it can even lead you
in the wrong direction.

But keep searching.

Eventually you will find

a familiar spark to follow.

That spark will show you the way back.

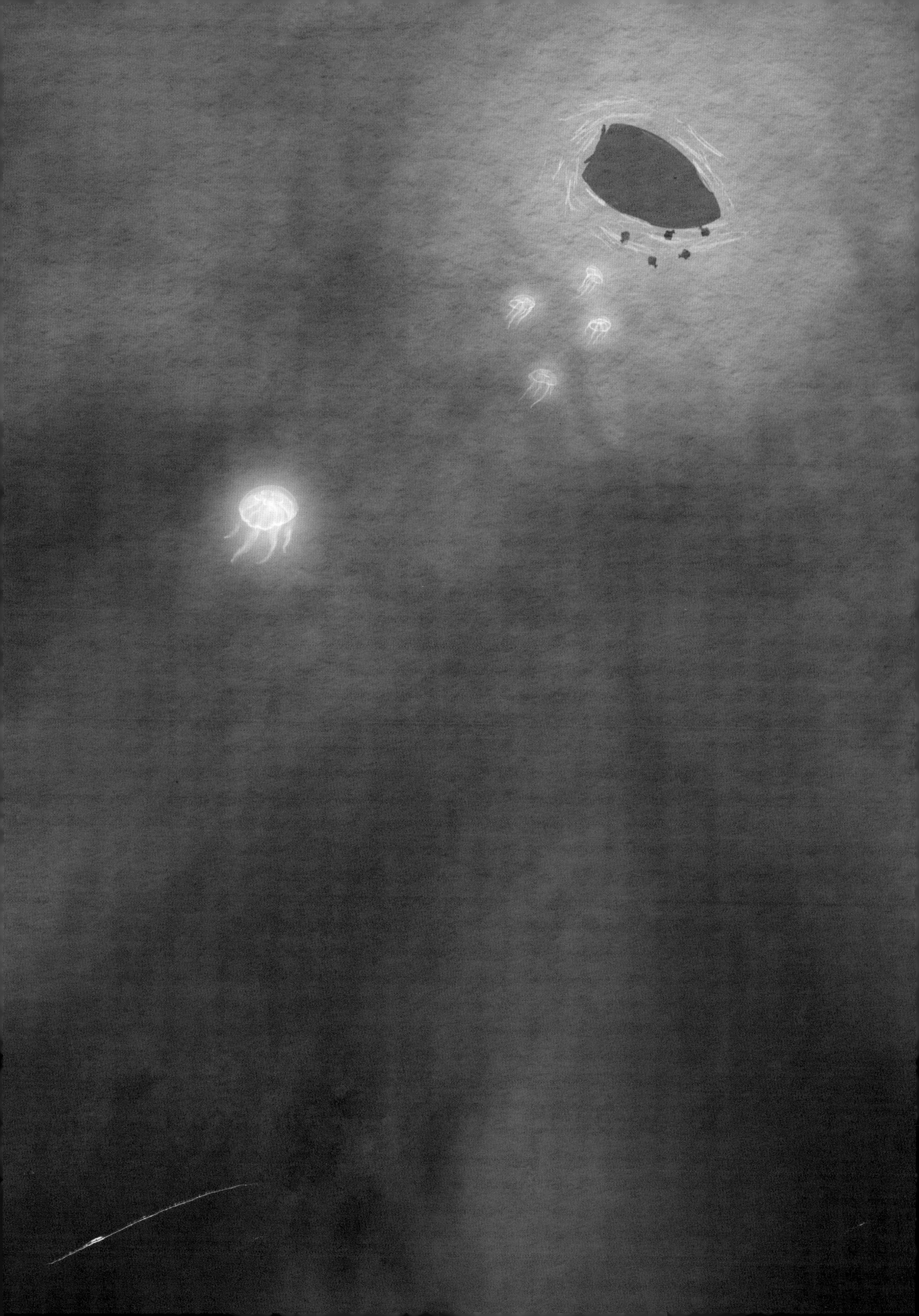

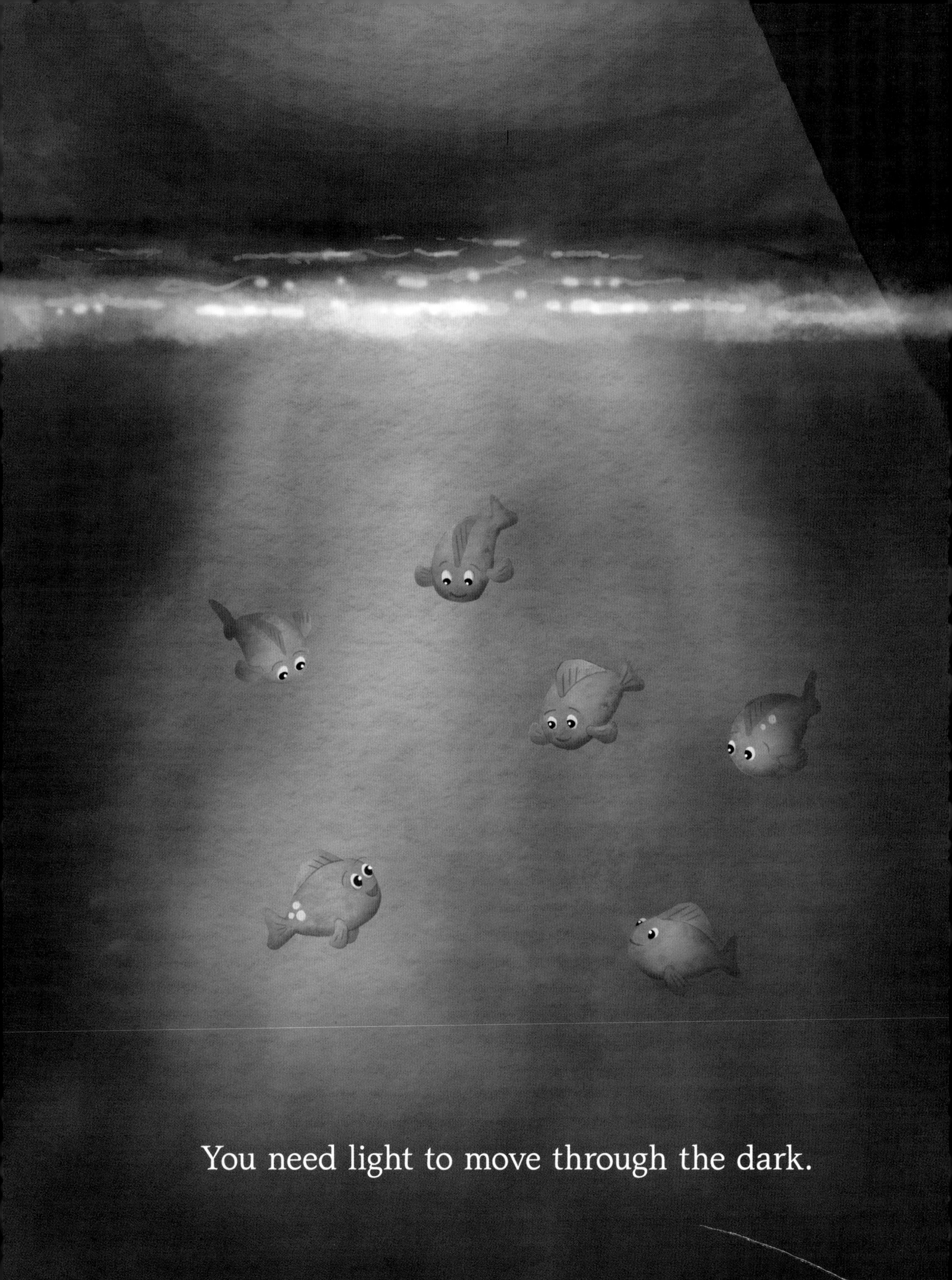

You need light to move through the dark.

But sometimes you need the dark . . .

to see the light.

For all those swimming in the dark

For information address HarperCollins Children's Books, a division of HarperCollins Publishers, 195 Broadway, New York, NY 10007.
www.harpercollinschildrens.com.
Full-colored artwork was created in watercolors and compiled digitally using Adobe Photoshop. The text type is 20-point Matte Antique BT.
Library of Congress Cataloging-in-Publication Data is available. ISBN 978-0-06-313653-3 (hardcover).
First Edition. 22 23 24 25 26 RTLO 10 9 8 7 6 5 4 3 2 1

Greenwillow Books